Henry Helps

with
the Dog

written by Beth Bracken   illustrated by Ailie Busby

PICTURE WINDOW BOOKS
a capstone imprint

Henry Helps books are published by Picture Window Books
A Capstone Imprint
1710 Roe Crest Drive
North Mankato, Minnesota 56003
www.capstonepub.com

Library of Congress Cataloging-in-Publication Data
Bracken, Beth.
Henry helps with the dog / by Beth Bracken ; illustrated by Ailie Busby.
p. cm. -- (Henry helps)
ISBN 978-1-4048-6771-0 (library binding)
ISBN 978-1-4048-7673-6 (paperback)
[1. Helpfulness--Fiction.] I. Busby, Ailie, ill. II. Title. III. Series.

PZ7.B6989Hep 2011
[E]--dc22
2010050101

Graphic Designer: Russell Griesmer
Creative Director: Heather Kindseth
Production Specialist: Michelle Biedscheid

Printed in the United States of America in North Mankato, Minnesota.
042018
000381

For Sam, the best helper I know. — BB

This is Henry's house.

Four people live in Henry's house.

But someone else lives there, too.

Toby lives there!

Toby is Henry's dog.

Henry helps Mom and Dad take care of Toby.

When it's time for Toby to eat,

Henry carefully pours dog food into a bowl.

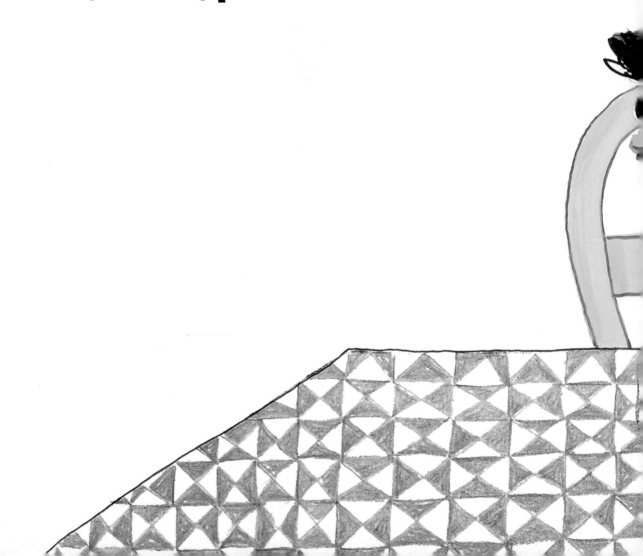

When Toby is thirsty,

Henry makes sure that he has enough water.

"Do you want to give Toby a treat?" Mom asks.

"Yes!" Henry yells.

When **Toby** wants to play,
Henry tosses him a ball.

When Toby needs a walk, Henry goes along.

"Look at the bunny!" Henry tells Toby.

After Toby takes a bath,

Henry dries him off.

And at night, when it's time for bed,
Toby curls up on the floor to help Henry sleep.

"Goodnight, Toby!" Henry whispers.